# WHITE RAVENS

## AND MORE STORIES

JIM STEWART

# WORD HERMIT PRESS LLC • USA

The following pieces in this collection were previously published:
"The Last Salmon" in *Rattapallax* 4, 2000
"And" in *Tulane Review*, 2013
"The Juggler" in *Portland Book Review*, 2013 (contest prize winner; 2nd place)
"The Cup" in *Progenitor*, 2013
"Early to Rise" as an Amazon Kindle book
"White Ravens" in *Mostly Maine*, 1998

Cover design: Vinnie Kinsella: Vinnie Kinsella Books
E-book ISBN: 978-1-7327508-1-4


Cataloging Information:
Stewart, James Richard (J.R.)
White Ravens: And More Sories
ISBN: 978-0-9982794-9-7
Recovery-Fiction
Relationship-Fiction
Psychology-Fiction
Travel-Fiction


Printed in the United States of America
For all inquiries: Word Hermit Press LLC, P.O. Box 20431, Charleston, SC 29413-0431

For Laura
and in memory of Brian Doyle

# STORIES

## THE LAST SALMON

She watched him from the window over the sink. The wind whipped his ponytail even as the rain tried to flatten it against his threadbare Levi jacket. Even wet, his hair was a bright gold rope beating on his back where it fell from beneath the dilapidated Cubs hat. She'd never seen the wind blow so hard, and watching him stand, seemingly unconcerned, in such a maelstrom scared her in a way she didn't understand.

His face was held in a frown of concentration as he studied the pile of scrap wood that had been accumulating from the odd jobs that he'd taken up and down this stretch of Oregon's North Coast. She didn't notice the long sigh that escaped her as he suddenly stooped and picked up a three-foot length of wood, tapered slightly from one end to the other. Even though they were each painfully aware of where the other was, he didn't so much as glance at the window as he disappeared from her line of sight, toward the work shed out back by the river.

Turning from the window, she reached for the dish towel and wiped her eyes. She felt a moment's panic when she considered that tomorrow was, indeed, Thanksgiving Day. She settled into her rocker by the woodstove and tried not to look at the phone.

Around back, he paused for a moment to watch the river. The wind, blasting out of the south, was pushing the surface of the water back upstream, like a flood tide. But he knew the tide was on its way out. This meant that the wind was blowing a pretty steady sixty, with gusts much higher than that. What a stupid time for an adventure. He cussed himself for his inability, sometimes, to find any middle ground at all.

The inside of the shed was calm. The rain beating on the roof was a friendly sound, but he knew that once the big front passed and the wind died some, the rain sound in here would be deafening. As it was, the wind was almost that way. He shuddered at the thought of what he was going to try, dicey at best even on a good day. Maybe this weather would be an ally instead. He snorted at the thought.

Clamping the piece of wood he'd chosen in the rust-pitted, but well-oiled vice, he rummaged for the eight-inch gutter spikes he knew he had. When he had them in hand, he picked up his framing hammer and commenced to work, grateful for something to do. When he was finished, he had what resembled a medieval mace, four of the spikes hammered at odd and forbidding angles through the thicker end of the wood.

On the way around the house to where his old 1964 Buick was parked, he willed himself not to look at any of the windows. He wanted no distraction from what he felt he had to do. Before tossing his new club into the trunk of the car, he swung it a few times and enjoyed a grim satisfaction in its heft and feel.

As the Buick turned south on 101, it was beginning to get dark. There was no traffic. The weather and tomorrow's holiday had most everyone hunkered down inside, waiting it out, anticipating the Big Meal, or maybe basking in the warm glow of a tavern, knowing that there would be plenty of time to shrug off a hangover.

His hands tightened on the wheel. Damn Thanksgiving dinner. He'd left her in the kitchen crying about Thanksgiving dinner. It was her first Thanksgiving away from home, and she couldn't bear the thought of not having a feast, of not having anything. He knew that she felt cut off, disconsolate, and there was nothing he could say to change it. As he'd pulled on his boots, face darkening like the sky outside, she'd looked at him, brown eyes huge and wet. His edge had disappeared like a sandbar in a rising tide, but he'd pretended it was still there, sharp as an axe.

"Where are you going?"

"To get tomorrow's dinner," he'd said as he stepped through the door onto the rain-lashed porch. Somebody had to do something. It might as well be him.

He stopped at the Chevron station in Wheeler and blew his last eight bucks on gas. Turning back onto the highway, he accelerated slowly, fighting the wind and the driven rain.

After a couple miles, the road dropped into a twisty hollow that was protected from the wind. He knew it was there still, roaring over the top, and he knew he'd be back in it as soon as he climbed out of there and crossed the railroad tracks near the end of the jetty that guarded the leeward river bank through the trees to his right. The relative quiet was welcome.

He passed through Neahkahnie and Rockaway, the Buick running smoothly, a good old dog eager to be going anywhere. Garibaldi came and went. The full force of the wind hit him as the road skirted the hills that crashed down to the ocean at where the road crossed the railroad tracks again. He expected traffic in Tillamook, but it was a ghost town, lights awash, signs bent straight to the northeast. At the only stoplight, he couldn't tell if it was green or red because it was little more than a flag in the gale. He went right on through without stopping.

As he went past the paper mill at the south end of town, it seemed to grow darker. It was right here, three weeks before, that things had started to fall. She'd been waiting in the car when he came out looking at the paper in his hand. Their eyes had met briefly through the windshield. When he'd settled into the seat, she'd said:

"Get your head up! Something else will come along."

He'd opened his mouth to say something, but her look had stopped him. His long sigh had been the only sound inside the car for the entire twenty-mile drive back up to Nehalem.

Now, he almost missed his turn. The flashing yellow light at the Trask River junction wasn't working. Maybe the power was out. All the better.

There were no lights, either, at the old blimp hangars that rose, unbelievably huge, out of the murk by the roadside, frightening somehow in their looming blackness. A fleet of loaded log trucks could park in either one of them and the place would still seem empty. For the first time, he noticed the knots in his stomach. He was about to break the law. He didn't care much about the state side of it. It was his own that troubled him.

Before he rounded what he knew was the last bend, he turned off the headlights and proceeded at a creep, tires crunching gravel on the road that followed the Trask up into the mountains. Driving more by feel than sight, he nosed off into a turnout he knew was there, nestled against the cliff that ran along the high side of the road. He turned the car around so that it was facing back the way he'd come. The wind was subdued up here, a distant howl. After he shut off the motor, the river became the dominant sound, eclipsing the rain that spattered against the convertible top and the windshield that was already beginning to fog.

He sat running it through his mind. Chances were excellent that no one would happen along, but he was still nervous, his heart hammering and his palms damp. It was cold, and he shivered, cursing himself for not having bought a winter coat when he'd had the money. And that was part of it. The money. Before he'd met her, it had never seemed like it was all that important. He got by, somehow, working here and there. Maybe carpentry one day, digging a ditch the next, helping out somewhere, always making the rent, almost always on time.

But somehow it had escaped, that feeling of being ready for anything, of knowing that his hands and his mind could provide a living. He knew it wasn't a living his father approved of, but it was his living. It was good enough until whatever it was that he was going to really do became apparent and led him off on another trail.

But then he'd met her. Now it was no longer good enough. He didn't know why. He just knew that it wasn't.

He got out of the car and the rain hit him. It was welcome. He was steady as he opened the trunk and got the club.

When he rounded the corner in the road, he saw a solitary light in the distance that marked where the people part of the hatchery was. No power outage here. Nothing stirred except the river, the rain, the high distant wind, and the beating of his heart. He stopped at the edge of the river where it pooled below the fish weir at the edge of the concrete where the hatchery began. The water was higher than he'd seen it before, but that made sense because of the storm. Even in the dark he could sense them there, hundreds of them, rolling and jostling one another in the black water.

Without hesitation, he stepped into the current and waded in up to his hips. The water was icy and pulled at him, turning his balls into a fist tight against him. He stood rock still and waited, letting himself calm and become part of the river. Rain pockmarked the sleek surface as he felt his legs grow numb. Soon he felt the first one brush against his legs, then another. When it was a constant bumping, he raised the spikes over his head and struck down with all his strength.

The river around him exploded, and the club almost tore itself from his hands. He held on with everything he had and backed slowly, a half step at a time, toward the bank. A rock rolled under his left foot, and he almost fell. Cursing as the cold was now over his belly, he kept the spikes downstream of the fish, so the current kept it impaled. When he recovered his balance and got close enough to the bank, he flipped the club, twenty pounds of salmon and all, up onto the road, where he pounced and held it with his knees while his knife cut the gills.

He washed his knife and his hands in the river, letting the fish bleed into the water. He felt a distant roaring in his ears, separate from the wind and rain and moving water. Just as he was about to get into the car, his head snapped high as his heart froze. Up at the hatchery buildings a door had slammed. When he heard the engine start, he leaped into the Buick and started his own.

How far could he get ahead before he could risk his headlights? He pictured the layout of the hatchery compound. He decided that he had maybe a thirty-second head start. If he could make it around a couple of curves, he could probably turn his lights on. But that left the long straightaway past the blimp hangars. There was no way he could get back to the highway before being seen.

Jaw set in a grim line, he knew that if he should even see the lights behind him, he was as good as busted. Headlights or not, he still needed his brakes, and their lights would give him away as sure as his headlights. So he turned them on and stomped the accelerator. The Buick shot forward, spewing gravel like shrapnel into the river.

He stayed ahead but knew there was no way he could make it to the highway without being seen. As he came around the big sweeping right-hand bend at the blimp hangars, he turned left, hard. The Buick slid down the long gravel apron that led into the first hangar. The headlights told him there was nothing parked inside for as far as he could see. When he was inside about a hundred yards, he turned off the lights and hammered his foot down on the parking brake. The Buick skidded sideways to a stop in the tarry dark as the unseen dust billowed around in a dense cloud.

Holding his breath, he waited for whoever was behind him to pass. It was a pickup, and he could just make out the Oregon Fish and Wildlife emblem painted on the door. Relief flooded him, releasing his shoulders and belly. He felt slightly dizzy as he sat in the vast blackness.

He counted as slowly as he could to two hundred before switching on his lights. Rolling down his window, he stuck his head out and looked up. The ceiling was only shadows at an impossible height. The rain was only a distant hum. The hangars were built in 1942 for the blimps that had been used as coastal defense and reconnaissance during World War II. In the seven-acre building, a football field wide and over a thousand feet long, he had no trouble turning the Buick around. Before he reached the yawning door, he turned off the headlights but left the parking lights on. Getting out of the car, he walked to the massive doorway and looked out. It was raining harder, but the wind seemed to have eased some. As he returned to the car, he noticed something laying in the shadows off to his right.

He walked over and nudged the shapeless mass with his boot. It was a coat. He couldn't begin to guess how long it had lain there. He picked it up and shook it out. It was a parka with a hood, down-filled and in good shape. There were no tears in it, and as he held it in the amber light of his parking lights, he felt a surge of thanks. As if in answer, he heard a thump from the Buick's trunk, the salmon making a last effort to swim, still hard-wired to fight anything that slowed it down. It had come so close to making it home.

He dug his flashlight from under the front seat and took the keys from the ignition. He opened the trunk and looked at the fish. The eyes were dull, and the chrome-bright skin was beginning to darken. He stood for a long time looking at the salmon, until the light from his flashlight began to yellow and fade.

"Thank you," he said and closed the trunk.

He made it back to the highway and turned north. The road was quiet for as far as he could see in both directions. He didn't pass another car until he was near the lonely station where he'd gassed up on the way down.

As soon as he opened the door, carrying the fish and his new coat, he knew that something was different. He also knew there was no going back. He found her note on the bed. She'd convinced her friend Ellen to take her to Portland. She was going home. She'd call in a couple of days.

He sat for a long time in the kitchen staring at the fish blood on his wet pants, wishing that he hadn't given up smoking. A wan smile crossed his face when he noticed the puddle on the floor under his boots. The kerosene lamp sputtered. He trimmed the wick, stood up, and took the fish down to the river. Someone had to clean it. It might as well be him.

Squatting in the water in the darkness at the base of the river bank, he poked the tip of his knife into the anus and gently slit open the long white belly. With a short yank, he cut through the hard cartilage near the gill plates and scooped out the guts with his hand. As dark as it was, he could still see the oily residue from the internal organs spread its sheen on the quiet water. As he washed his fish at the edge of his river, he vowed that this would be the last salmon he would ever take.

## AND

A languor creeps upon him, and the buzzing stops, almost. If it doesn't stop, it is suddenly transported to the far reaches of himself, and it seems unimportant to acknowledge its presence. He remembers having pain, but not the pain itself, the sharp cut and burn trailing through his spine and along his legs. It is far away, gone with the eyedropper and the short, cool squirt under his tongue, bitter yet strangely sweet. Lips brush his forehead, and he realizes that his hands are being held, one on each side of the narrow bed. He smiles.

A rush of wings engulfs him, and a crow sits on a small altar of rock, her head cocked, watching him with a glittering obsidian eye. Wind ruffles his hair.

"You are here," says the crow.

"I am everywhere," he says, surprised at the strength of his own voice.

The crow rattles with laughter. "Not quite yet," she says, "but yes, it is coming to that."

He feels a warm surge of gratitude, as if every molecule in his being were giving thanks for the world. His heart unleashes a torrent, a vast waterfall of feeling and

The toboggan picked up speed quickly on the upper slope and gathered momentum. He was lying on his big brother's back, holding tight to the hood of Tom's parka, his heart charged with a sparkling excitement.

At the bottom of the hill, the river coursed through the hilly meadow, a clear expanse of white in the late-afternoon sun. The toboggan had started to slow a bit, but when they hit the ice, their speed picked up immediately, and they shot across the flat surface. The goal was to reach the other side. The boys did not hear the booming crack with the wind in their ears and their stocking caps pulled down tight.

The toboggan slowed and finally stopped, ten yards from the opposite shore. The wind had cleared the snow from where they were, and they rolled off the long flat sled onto the black of the ice. Standing up was a slippery dance.

As they trudged back across the river, footing was easier because of the new snow. His brother dragged the toboggan behind them. "You want to try it again, little buddy?" Tom asked.

His feelings were mixed. "Dad said we should stay off the river for another week to let the ice get really thick," he said.

"Yeah, I know," Tom said, "but it's fine." He stomped his boots to make his point.

A crack appeared immediately between Tom's legs, and the ice began to give way beneath them. There came a wrenching cracking and screeching as the surface changed. Tom disappeared, swallowed by roiling black water. He heard a plaintive scream but didn't know it was his own. He lay on the broken ice, his legs in the water at his knees, and his torso across the toboggan. The noise of the water was a menacing murmur tearing at his heart. Consciousness slipped from his grasp like a thread of mercury from a glass cup.

He awoke to a snuffling whine and a wet nose in his left ear. He felt the dog grip his parka collar and try to drag him away from the open water. He tried to help but his body wouldn't obey.

"Tommy," he sobbed.

His jeans were frozen stiff, and he felt himself sliding, inch by inch, away from the jagged hole in the ice. The dog's breath in his ear was thunderous. The parka gathered under his chin and began to choke him as the dog pulled. He didn't care. His legs burned and—

"Do you remember the dog?" the crow asks.

His rush of gratitude pauses. "Yes. It was the skinny old Irish setter that didn't seem to belong to anybody. He dragged me to solid ice and then lay on me so I wouldn't freeze to death. After that day, I never saw him again."

"Sure you did," rattles the crow, as merry as she can be. "Think about it."

He feels a flash of impatience, but suddenly, he was in Vietnam, crouched in a stand of mulberry. He was desperately afraid, hidden by a log as a column of black-clad men moved past him, not thirty feet away, talking casually and carrying rifles. He could not believe they didn't hear the heart hammering in his ears.

He'd been separated from his unit during an ambush and lost his orientation. When the column of Charlie had passed, he started breathing again and wondered which way he should go. He decided to follow the trail Charlie had been using, but in the opposite direction. He'd been just about to start out when a wild red dog, a dhole, loped from the woods and sat staring at him. Something about the way the dog's head was cocked, and his frank, penetrating stare, pierced his fear. He followed as the dog trotted off, perpendicular to the trail he'd first decided on. Within fifteen minutes, he reunited with his sergeant and his buddies. They'd survived the ambush with a couple of bloody soft-tissue wounds but were whole other than that. It was only then that he noticed that he was bleeding from a hot crease in his scalp.

"Man," Sarge said, "we thought you were gone. Chopper's coming two klicks south. C'mon, gotta go."

He never did tell them about the wild red dog. He wasn't sure he believed it himself.

Years later, he told the story to his wife and children, who accepted it at face value. Nobody sought to explain it away with some logical theory.

"No wonder you give to animal shelters every Christmas" was all his wife said.

His kids thought it odd but cool at the same time.

"Dad," they said, "you're weird, but it's a good weird."

He remembered beaming with a feeling of something almost, but not exactly, like pride. He still didn't know what to think of both stories. He felt certain that it didn't matter what he thought.

"Why?" he asks the crow.

"Pay attention," she says and spreads her shining blue-black wings to lift herself from the stone.

The narrow bed presses against his spine. Warmth engulfs his hands. He tries to squeeze back and hears his daughter's voice.

"Did you feel that?"

He hears his son answer: "Yes."

After a moment of silence, his son's voice breaks through again. "We love you, Pop."

"Yes," his daughter says.

He squeezes his hands as hard as he can and feels, again, a brush of lips against his forehead.

"See?" says the crow, gliding above him. "Each has made the world a better place, as you did. It goes on."

He doesn't know what to say as the crow vanishes and he stands in a wooded glen. A dog with a shining coat of glossy red runs to him, full of happy wag, and—

BLEEDING ALDER

*Author's note: The main character in this story is a much younger version of Mike Ironwood, who carries the action in Ochoco Reach, my debut novel from Word Hermit Press.*

The radio barked something unintelligible and scared the crap out of me. It had been a quiet January day of intermittent rain and blustery winds. For me, it had been surging along very slowly. I was covering Clatsop County in my white 1972 Plymouth that said, Oregon State Police, on its front doors. My usual beat was on the other side of the Cascades, along I-84 as far east as Boardman and south down into Wasco, Sherman, Gilliam, Morrow, and Umatilla Counties. My friend Thad Krieger had needed a few days off so he and his wife could visit family down in Medford, and I'd agreed to cover for him.

I liked the lonely country in Oregon's northwest corner, where the Columbia River emptied eastern British Columbia, Washington, Oregon, Idaho, and some of Montana into the Pacific. As far as employment went, logging was king. Other trades flourished too, mostly fishing and construction. Tourism was also big and getting bigger.

I didn't mind the wet but was glad I hadn't had to spend much time outside of my warm, dry cruiser. I'd had enough soaking in Vietnam.

The radio crackled again. I was ready for it this time.

"Dead deer reported on 101 near Sunset Lake. Twenty-four, can you respond?"

It took me a second to realize the dispatcher was talking to me. I keyed my mic.

"Ten-four, this is twenty-four. I'll go take a look."

Usually, the county sheriff would coordinate cleanup, but I was pretty close, so it made sense for me to respond. I'd just passed through Gearhart and was nosing into Seaside when the call came in. I used the high school to turn around and headed north, back up US 101.

Like most rural areas of any state, roadkill was a way of life. It was generally illegal for the public to mess with it, so it fell to law enforcement and private contractors to clean it up.

Once past Gearhart, I let the horses run a little, and my Plymouth hummed along nicely. It didn't take me long to reach the road that went west toward Sunset Lake. I passed an old beater pickup coming the other way. In the dim, rainy afternoon, I saw that one of his headlights was out and heard him shift into third. Must have turned onto the highway from Sunset Lake.

I scanned both sides of the highway and did not see a deer. I called in. "This is twenty-four. Ten-twenty and no deer."

"Don't know what to tell you," the dispatcher said. "The caller said the buck was on the west side about fifty yards south of the Sunset Lake road."

I turned around and looked more closely. I did see an antler lying at the far edge of the gravel strip by the side of the road. The left side, I thought. But no deer. I crept along and stopped, flipped on my rack lights, and examined the ground. There had been something there. There was blood. I could also see drag marks.

I got back in my cruiser, turned off the roof lights, and put the hammer down. I don't like lights or sirens unless I need them. I didn't feel that urgency. I was, however, curious. As if on cue, a distant drumming started in me, not exactly in my head, more like a pulse I couldn't define that resonated all through me. I did my best to ignore it, but it always made me curious. My brother, Daniel, and I shared a father but had different mothers. His was full-blooded Nez Perce. When we were teenagers, I'd told him about the drumming and the voices I sometimes heard. He'd just nodded like it was the most natural thing in the world. We'd both served in Vietnam, Daniel as a SEAL and me as a Green Beret. I'd mustered out a few years ago, but he was still gallivanting around the world, serving his country and avoiding civilian life. Our father still ran the home ranch, Iron Wood, high up in the Blue Mountains out of Ukiah. I tried to accept my internal sounds as matter-of-factly as my brother did, but it was difficult.

I keyed the mic. "Twenty-four. Proceeding south, Cold."

"Ten-four," came the response.

As I swept around the gentle curve past the south end of Del Moor Loop, I saw taillights at the far end of the straightaway where Gearhart started. I goosed the throttle a little and grinned to myself. I was pretty sure I knew where the deer was.

The law is the law, and it was my job to enforce it. But working rural Oregon gave me the opportunity to think a lot, and I argued with myself constantly about the letter of the law and the spirit of the law. Did circumstances make a difference? For me, roadkill was a gray area. What did it hurt if somebody was able to get some meat off the highway? I figured that anybody who took the trouble to pick a dead animal off the road wasn't doing so out of boredom or malicious intent. No. They were taking it home as food, probably needed food. The spirit part of the law was to protect people from poisoning themselves, from putting themselves in harm's way from food-borne illness. The letter part of the law didn't care a whit about that.

I grew up in rural Oregon's Blue Mountains and couldn't think of a single person I knew in my old community who didn't know their way around a carcass and always understood good meat from bad. As teenagers, Daniel and I had prepared roadkill and eaten it ourselves, just to see if we could do it. We could. Venison with wild onions and greens: it was a fine meal.

But laws in Oregon are mostly made by those living in the urban parts of the Willamette Valley. Because of population, those folks had more representation than the rest of the state combined. They had different cares and different issues. Sometimes, what was common sense in the mountains, on the broad plains, and on the beach became illegal just because those in the valley thought a law was a good idea and didn't think of their fellow citizens elsewhere.

I was gaining quickly. I figured I'd catch the truck right about at the drive-in theater, but it turned right, off 101, onto the road that wrapped itself around the golf course. I tried to minimize the drama of it but followed quickly, only drifting my tires briefly, and flipped on my lights. Dammit, it was fun to control a good automobile as it drifted. I had to admit that Vietnam had done nothing to curtail my enjoyment of adrenalin. The old truck, a beat-up early-'60s Ford F100, pulled over immediately, considerately coming to a stop well off the road. I was right behind him.

"Ten eighty-four," I said into my mic. "Ten twenty-eight for Oregon 028TYU."

"Ten-four," came the reply.

As I waited, I gathered my broad-brimmed hat. As usual, I was growing tired of the ten codes. I much preferred English.

"Registered to Martin Donovan, 105 Avenue C, Gearhart. No warrants or outstanding issues."

"Martin Donovan? The writer?"

There was a pause. "I have no idea."

At least it was English.

I got out of the Plymouth, careful that my hat didn't fly off in the southwesterly wind. Martin Donovan wrote novels I liked very much. They were stories of how Oregon became Oregon, how the native people, Daniel's ancestors, dealt with the interlopers, my ancestors. They were powerful and true, and I'd learned many things from each book. The sweep of his prose was hard to put down. I'd known he lived on the Oregon coast. The coincidence was too great. Had to be him.

The bed of the truck was filled with firewood, alder it looked like. There was no deer visible. But I smelled blood, something that had become a survival skill during my time in Southeast Asia.

I approached cautiously, with my hand resting lightly on my Smith & Wesson 1911. It didn't speak much outside of the practice range, but when it did, it spoke with authority. I saw the glint of glasses in the driver-side mirror. As I got close, the window rolled down. A hand held out a license and registration.

"Thank you," I said.

I peered into the cab. The face looking back at me was haggard and fleshy and had a three-day stubble, like a Christmas wreath that had been left hanging too long. It was a very worried face. I couldn't blame him for that. I put myself in his seat and decided I'd be worried too.

"The reason I pulled you over is your right-front headlight is out. You need to get it fixed."

"I know it," he said. "I noticed it this morning but had too much to do, so I haven't fixed it yet. And I'm waiting on a check to show up. It's late, and I have to fix dinner for the kids. I'll go to the parts store tomorrow and get it done."

"You the writer?"

His eyebrows dropped as his eyes narrowed. "Yeah." It was almost a question.

"I admire your work, Mr. Donovan. It's given me great pleasure."

He smiled like a kid. "Really? Sometimes I forget people actually read."

I smiled back. "Nice load of alder."

The kid left his face, and the old man returned. His lower dentures didn't fit very well. "Yeah. Got it up outside of Knappa. It's sorely needed. Been a tough winter so far."

The rain was beating my hat like Ginger Baker.

"Hang on a sec. I'm gonna write you a warning for the headlight. When it's fixed, you can find any cop, prove it to him, and he'll sign off on the warning. Just mail it to Astoria, and it'll be a done deal."

I heard him roll up the window as I trudged back to my car. I got in and wrote up the warning. I really did like his writing. The author photo on his books must be from long ago. Why was anyone with his talent hauling a dead deer home for food? It didn't seem fair.

This time I had to tap on his window to let him know I was there. The glass lowered. I handed him back his license and registration, along with the written warning in its little metal box.

"Like I said, get the light fixed and find an officer to sign off. Just sign at the bottom, please. The address where to send it is on the ticket."

"Okay."

He handed the book in its metal case back to me. I tore off his copy, handed it to him, and tucked the box under my left arm.

"And you know the badass guy in 'The Gray Hills of Winter,' the guy who just vanishes after causing so much grief? I've always wondered where he went."

"You must have read it when you were younger." Donovan laughed. "Read it again. You'll figure it out." He paused a second. "What's your name, if you don't mind my asking."

"Mike Ironwood. Nice to meet you Mr. Donovan." I held out my hand.

After we shook, he nodded, eager to be gone, and started to roll up his window.

"Oh, and Mr. Donovan…"

He paused and stared at me through the rain, jaw tight against that loose denture.

"You'd best get that load of alder home before it bleeds to death."

I walked back to my car and sat in it, dripping, as he drove away. I'd had to let him know I knew. Next time, he'd better understand the risk. I turned around and drove back to 101, hoping I was a good cop.

## THE JUGGLER

He juggles three oranges as he walks the length of the short pier. As he stares into the distant space between the oranges, his careful bare feet watch for jagged boards and hot bolt heads. The sun weighs on his back and throws a small shadow beneath his bare legs as he moves.

He can smell the bait that the fishermen are using. It is a community bucket with a stained white towel thrown over it to keep the overhead sun from cooking the small fry in it. By this time of day, the odor is unavoidable. The men are fanned out at the end of the pier, separated by the lengths of their poles and the arcs of their casts.

A scrawny dog sleeps in the only shade available, a thin shadow cast by the one-hole outhouse that precariously sits at the port side of the pier. It squats on the seaward side of the mean high-tide line. Whatever lands below is washed out to sea twice a day. When the dog sees the juggler, he thumps his skinny tail.

The fishermen wait until the oranges stop their circular weaving before addressing the stocky, well-made juggler.

"*Hola, Amigo,*" says their spokesman, "*que pasa?*"

The juggler answers in soft Spanish with a gringo accent. "I am well, thank you, Jorge. Has God smiled on your fishing fortunes today?"

Jorge smiles and looks at his companions. "A little bit," he says. "I think we all have dinner."

"Excellent," says the juggler. "Please accept two oranges to share. I cannot eat them all."

"Thank you, Juglar. Would you like a fish today?"

"No, you are too kind. Perhaps another day, if I may."

"Certainly," says Jorge as he takes two oranges and tosses one to his friend down the short row of dark wiry men. It is a good throw, but the man misjudges it, and the orange takes an odd bounce out of his hand and falls over the edge of the railing.

It is barely out of sight before the juggler puts his last orange on the railing next to him and launches himself from the pier. He cuts cleanly into the water twenty feet below, barely a second after the orange.

The fishermen let out a collective gasp and lean over the railing, their fishing poles forgotten. A quiet panic fills them as they wait for the juggler to reappear. A few seconds later, they see him explode to the surface in a froth of white bubbles and smooth his long sun-bleached hair away from his face. He holds up the orange for them to see and laughs at their astonished faces. His blue eyes are alive with excitement.

"Be right up," he says and tucks the orange into the netting of his faded blue swim trunks.

He swims around the side of the pier away from the outhouse with strong, sure strokes. The fishermen watch him with amazement.

"We should call him Nadador," says Jorge. "He swims better than he juggles."

The others murmur in agreement and wonder how the juggler seems to do everything so swiftly. They go back to their fishing until they hear the quiet slap of bare feet jogging up the pier toward them. The dog thumps his tail again. They turn toward the sound, glancing sheepishly at one another. The juggler, carrying the orange, has a big smile on his face. His eyes look like turquoise against the caramel of his skin.

When he stops, he grabs the orange he left on the railing and tosses it into the air. Soon, both oranges are circling his head. It almost makes the fishermen dizzy.

"Pedro," he says to Jorge's friend who missed the orange, "be ready."

Pedro puts down his pole and tries to be ready. When one orange magically flies in his direction, he catches it and holds on. The juggler catches the remaining orange and holds it still. Everyone breathes a sign of relief.

The juggler's hair is gathered into a ponytail and drips down his back into his trunks. His sturdy legs are still wet.

"I must go," he says and looks at Jorge. "May I give your dog the treat I have in my pocket? I do not think he will mind a little salt water."

Jorge smiles. "Of course," he says. It will complete the ritual.

The juggler smiles back. "Until tomorrow, my friends," he says.

The dog has moved, following the shadow as it snakes around the outhouse. The juggler reaches into his pocket as he squats by the dog, who raises his head to take the treat. He allows his ears to be scratched and thumps his tail again.

The juggler stands and, with a final wave to the fishermen, strides back toward the shore along the rough planks. The fishermen watch him go for a few seconds and then turn back to the sea and their fishing.

Jorge and Pedro peel their oranges to share with the others.

"I do not think he gave me back the same orange that fell into the sea," Pedro says.

"He is a very strange man," says Jorge. "He may even be crazy. But I like him."

"I do also," says Pedro as the others nod.

The orange peels fall into the water below where the Garibaldi goldfish peck at them. They think the peels are like themselves.

## THE CUP

The fire flared and startled him away from a place that he couldn't remember as soon as he realized he wasn't actually there. He stood up and discovered that his left foot was asleep. Staggering slightly, he tossed the last cold quarter-inch of his coffee and whiskey against the poor drunken scrub pine that leaned like it was trying to escape the repeated dousing and the heat of the fire.

In the shadows away from the fire, the air was smokeless and cold, washed by the wind and the river moving swiftly by. Moving to the five-gallon jug he'd set up by the stove, he rinsed his cup and put it, upside down, over the top of one of the aluminum poles that held up the front of the tarp that he'd rigged over the cooking area. He yawned hugely. He looked at the cup. He put it exactly there whenever he was out like this. It made a camp feel like home. Or how he imagined home to feel.

He was brushing his teeth when he had to admit that he was drunk. Not roaring drunk, or bad hangover drunk, but drunk nonetheless. It became apparent when he spit the long stream of white foam out onto his boot. Chuckling, he mocked himself by staggering to the tent, removing all of his clothes, and flopping in a stage-clumsy way onto the big foam pad where his sleeping bag waited. He was snoring in minutes.

He awoke with a start and wondered why. Maybe it was too quiet. Even the river seemed muted as it moved on down its chute, down to Bend, past Warm Springs and Maupin, over Sherar's Falls to wind past Grass Valley, through Macks Canyon, to forgotten Moody above where Celilo had disappeared, to marry the Columbia and help spin the turbines, and finally out across The Bar where ships and bones sleep in the deep cold dark.

He heard it begin somewhere down the canyon. Wind in the trees. He felt the air in the tent pause and gather itself before the rainfly began to chatter and buck. He heard the rolling snap of the tarp over the cooking area. The ancient ponderosas around the tent creaked and groaned as their backs stretched and turned. The gust died briefly but finished with a very strong blow that buckled and snapped all the fabric he'd diligently erected. This flurry was strong enough to give him a small thrill of fear.

He wanted to drift back to sleep, but then he remembered the cup. "Damn!" He knew he had to get up. He'd never forgive himself if the cup didn't survive this wind. It had survived other blows, but he had a feeling about this one. The cup had been a gift and had traveled in his camp box since that desert night when the sky was bigger and the shooting stars brighter than any other night he could call to memory. It had been their first trip together. She had presented him with coffee in the new cup before bed that first evening.

"Jeez, lady," he'd said. "You trying to keep me awake?"

"You can be awake if you want to be," she'd shot back. "I'm more concerned with keeping you up."

It was a joke they'd shared until the sky streaked with light and the roadrunners improvised their peculiar morning song. They drifted somewhere close to sleep as the sun rose and stayed abed until it got too hot. They could have stayed longer had they been lying separately, but each was unwilling to sacrifice the long, smooth heat of the other. They reveled in their glorious soreness, breathing the same air and talking through gentle bruised lips.

The cup was all he had left. She'd gone her bittersweet way in Bishop at Christmastime that following winter. She was headed back to Kansas to see her mom and said that she'd come find him in the spring. But they both knew. All he said was: "I'll be in Oregon, I think."

He didn't bother to get dressed. The windchill caught his attention, but it was more invigorating than painful. He was now grateful for the whiskey burning those empty calories that made him feel warm. Still, his breath plumed briefly before the wind snatched it from his lips. He almost got to the tarp before another gust put in it a big belly that stretched for the sky. He watched the cup dance on its pole.

The rain took him by surprise and wrapped him in a thin membrane. A knot began to form at the base of his neck. He felt it when he reached for the cup. The mere touch of it took him back to the desert, as it always did. Where was she? Did she ever have those children that she'd wanted? Probably. They'd be in school now and would climb into her lap for a good story when they got home, a story that revealed the magic of just being alive, of being a person who loved with the whole heart and was loved in a careful, complete way by a special person, of having skin to stroke and kiss. God, could she tell a story. With a few simple words she could show how things were, how they grew, how you wanted them to be.

The familiar ache of it stuck him now, but he knew what to do. He turned to the tent where he could dry off and meticulously fish tomorrow's water until he fell asleep. But the whiskey and his right foot betrayed him. He tripped hard against an upright chunk of firewood that had served as his stool while he'd sat drinking before the fire. He watched the cup fly from his hands and, in slow motion, strike the base of the concrete firepit. It bounced in the air and made a half turn before it separated neatly into two halves. The handle left in a third stage, and it all came to rest in a scatter that transfixed him.

As his foot throbbed in the distance, he stared at the pieces as the rain came down. After a while, he began to shiver.

He caught no fish the next day, or the day after. He ran out of bait before he ran out of hooks, but it was a close race. On the third day, he switched to the fly rod, but the big browns lurked in the snags and sunken trees, which made it difficult fishing. Finally exasperated, he went back to camp and packed his stuff.

The pieces of the cup still lay on the scarred camp table where he'd left them. Before packing the stove, he made some coffee and poured it into the tin cup he'd had before meeting her. The coffee tasted dusty and strange. There was no whiskey to add to it, and he didn't want any. He rummaged in his vest for a cigar, snipped the end, and lit it. Walking back down to the river, he sat smoking on a rock that was still in the sun. He did his best to think of exactly nothing.

When he pulled out of camp an hour later, he headed north with the river. The cup stayed where it was, pieces reflecting the morning sun. As the clatter of the truck receded, a crow flew in and settled on the table. Cocking her head, she eyed the glinting handle. Taking the shiny curve in her beak, she spread her wings and flew upriver, away from the noise.

EARLY TO RISE

*Authors note: Willy, in this story, became Willamina Hayes, the love of Mike Ironwood's life in my novel Ochoco Reach. This is where she began in my mind. Like other characters of mine, she appeared unbidden. I had no idea she was coming when I sat down that day to work on the story.*

When Jack awoke, he had only the briefest of thoughts before he fell into the hole.

The hole was in the middle of him somewhere. Sometimes it was where his heart used to be, and sometimes it moved to his belly, where it churned like a mixer in raw dough.

Her name came to him. Sarah. And the hole expanded to encompass all of him. He was falling without center, turning and tumbling in a limitless expanse. There was pain, to be sure, and remorse and hopelessness all rolled into a spiraling emptiness that was in the unending act of swallowing him whole.

He ignored the anger that hid behind the guilt until he heard the baby wake up and begin to cry. Then the flash of anger burst incandescent, and he closed his eyes until it passed. He drew a long shuddering breath, and the hole shrank until it was just an ache in his chest that he could almost manage.

He got out of bed and pulled on a pair of undershorts. The elastic band snapped against the taut tanned skin as he moved to the bassinet that occupied one corner of the plain gray room. His huge callused hands smoothed the tiny brow, and as he gazed at his daughter and smiled, the hole within him almost disappeared.

He carried her out of the bedroom and into the kitchen where his feet unconsciously tried to avoid the cracks in the linoleum floor. The hole seized this small opportunity and tried to take him over again, tried to convince him that if he'd just taken the time to put down new linoleum that Sarah would still be here. But he knew this to be a lie, which pointed at a deeper and darker truth.

"Early to bed, early to rise, and your girl goes out with other guys." It was an old saw, one that he'd laughed at as a boy. It didn't seem quite so funny now.

"The early bird gets the worm." He laughed humorlessly to himself as his daughter nestled in an orange blanket against the inadequate flat planes of his wide chest. She stopped her fussing as he watched her nurse from the bottle. After a time, she let the nipple pop out of her mouth and sighed, a breath of deep contentment that he openly envied.

Jack changed her diaper, and then she wanted to eat again. He supposed, as he watched her face in the pale gray light, that she had his broad forehead and wide nose. It was too soon to tell about her eyes. But she definitely had her mother's mouth, full and soft and shaped like a heart. He felt a rush of shame as he thought of her mother's mouth, sucking just like the mouth of this tiny daughter, but even more insistently and with a hunger that was never entirely satisfied. But the total concentration, the primal need, they were exactly the same.

The baby reached up with a tiny hand and pushed the bottle away. Her eyes were open and gazed frankly into his.

"Hi," she seemed to say. "You're familiar, but who are you?"

"I'm your daddy, and I love you."

"I know you do, but you're not all here. Where's the rest of you?"

He felt himself hesitate, unwilling to continue with the game. But he knew that maybe it wasn't just a game. Maybe he was crazy, at least losing his grip. But maybe too, he'd found a way to begin filling the hole.

"I think," the thought stammered slightly, "that the rest of me is with your mother."

"My mother?"

"Yes. Your mother gave you life. You lived inside of her until you came out to breathe the air."

"Oh, I remember. It seems so far away. She didn't really care, you know."

A band of sunlight appeared on the beige wall above his head.

"My mother is gone?"

He swallowed.

"Yes. She ran away with a trumpet player."

"What's a trumpet player?"

"It's not important. A man. Like me, but different."

"But what's left of you is here with me?"

"Yes."

"For always?"

"Yes."

"Then I think my mother is just a place where I lived for a while and now it's gone and I'm with you."

"You might feel different about that when you're older."

"Maybe. But it's not important now."

"No. I don't suppose it is right now."

"But Daddy, what is important is that you're not all here. I think I need all of you."

He felt tears trying to escape.

"I know. I need to find the rest of me."

"Did my mother take it?"

"No, I think I let her have it."

"You need to get it back."

The sunlight lit his unruly dark hair now as he sat transfixed by the eyes of the child.

"Daddy, what's my name?"

"Lisha. That's what I call you. Your big name is Alecia Jane Robbins."

"Lisha. I like it. What was my mother's name?"

"Sarah. Her name is Sarah."

"You need to go find Sarah and get the rest of you back. I need all of you and so do you."

He paced the floor with her against his shoulder, thinking about how to do it, how to find them and close the open book. After a while, he knew how to find them. He wasn't at all sure of what to do when he did, but he trusted himself to know when the time came.

"Lisha?"

The silence grew.

"Lisha?"

He brought her away from his shoulder, and the sunlight played there on her calm face. There was a smile on her little heart of a mouth. He put her back in the bassinet and then made a couple of phone calls. Satisfied that he'd covered all his bases, Jack went outside, sat on the front steps, and enjoyed the morning for the first time in a long time. He still felt the hole in his center, but for the first time, he noticed that it had walls.

Later, when the sun had been above the low line of hills to the east for a couple hours and the smell of the sea filled the emptiness of the small house, Jack awakened Lisha, changed her, fed her again, and pushed the stroller up the street to Eunice, her babysitter.

"You be careful, Jack," Eunice said from the screen door as he walked down the drive. "That Peterson boy can be real bad, especially when he's been drinking."

Jack turned.

"Thanks, Eunice. I will. I'm not looking for trouble, I'm looking for a place to lay it down. And thanks a lot for helping me out like this. I'll be in touch."

"Don't worry about your girl. She'll be fine. You go do what you need to do."


After breakfast and a long walk along the cliffs above the ocean, he got down to it. The trail was three months cold, but it only took him a couple hours to get a lead. Jack had been right when he'd figured that a trumpet player with an attitude wouldn't be too hard to track. The clubs that featured live music in the evenings were just beginning to open, exchanging the smoke and passion of the night before with the fresh air and sunlight of a new day. In the fourth club he tried, he found a sad-eyed drummer who knew Pete Peterson.

"Yeah, sure," the drummer said while eyeing the beer in front of him like he would a friend with whom he'd recently argued, "I know Pete. Last I heard, him and his girlfriend went up to a gig in Bakersfield." He tapped out a rhythm on the bar.

"How long ago?"

"'Bout two weeks."

"You know what club?"

"Naw, but it weren't one of the big ones. Pete's got the chops to play, you know? But he don't have the right attitude. Like, he figures he should start out at the top instead of paying his dues. He once told me that paying dues was for chumps."

The drummer took a long pull on the beer and tapped at the bar with the thumb and fingers of his free hand.

"Say," he asked. "Why're you looking for Pete anyways?"

"His girlfriend's got something of mine, and I want it back."

Tap. Tap. Tap.

"Okay. You be careful. Pete's okay when he sober. He's not when he's not. And he carries a gun, one of those S&W thirty-eight Specials. Clips it on his left hip with the handle pointed forward. The girlfriend doesn't like it, says it makes her feel strange."

"Talk to her much, did you?"

"Naw, not much" Tappity-tappity-tap. "She's a real nice-looking blond girl, looks like she could be a dancer. Sarah, I think her name was. I liked her, but she kept going on about Van Gogh and the 'artist temperament'"—he pronounced it arteest with a wave of his hand—"so I kind of tuned her out. Nice girl, though. What's she got of yours anyway?"

Jack flipped a couple dollars up onto the bar.

"Thanks. The next one's on me too."

He got up, walked out of the door into the bright sunlight, and stood blinking in the parking lot. Jack was very careful not to fall into the hole that was yawning around him as he went home and grabbed a few clothes and his shaving kit. Then he hit the bank machine and pointed his battered green Chevy pickup at Bakersfield, some hundred and forty miles to the north.

The front end of the truck had a shimmy that disappeared above sixty-five, so Jack kept it at seventy as he rolled through the depressing brown goo that had begun to ooze even into the seaward valleys from the LA Basin. He was mildly amused at the drummer's recollection of Sarah's Van Gogh fixation. The guy didn't know the half of it.

He remembered awakening several times during the night as Sarah traced the curve of his ear lightly with her fingertips. Sometimes he'd responded, and sometimes he'd pretended to still be asleep. He wondered, though, just what had been going through her head at those times. On those mornings that followed, she'd invariably asked him if he'd ever considered getting a tattoo. He'd always laughed and said no. He just couldn't figure it out.

Then about a year ago, he'd received a clue. Out of the blue, after making love, she'd asked him a truly strange question.

"Would you cut your ear off for me if you had to? I mean if you really had to?"

"Why would I ever have to? That's ridiculous."

She'd fallen silent then, and the subject had never come up again. But—he eased back on the throttle as a black-and-white shot past on the right—he'd noticed a subtle change in her after that. She'd started taking down her Van Gogh prints and storing them away. He'd never asked her about it. He'd been afraid to. Maybe if he'd been able to ask, things would be different.

Carefully, he steered around the hole and pulled over into the line of traffic that was speeding to join Interstate 5.

The dusty grayness of Bakersfield settled around him quickly, and he remembered his dad saying, "Never trust air you can see." Jack stopped at the first honky-tonk he saw and sat with a beer and the Yellow Pages, trying to develop a plan. There were a few folks scattered about the room, mostly in pairs, waiting for the scene to begin. It was still some hours until the music started.

Jack finally decided that he didn't need much of a plan. After all, he wasn't trying to sneak up on anybody—he was just trying to make contact.

At the third club he tried, a place on Chester Avenue called Lefty's, Jack found a waitress who had no trouble remembering the couple.

"Oh yeah, they were here all right." She laughed a smoky laugh and jangled her silver bracelets as she smoothed her shining red hair. "He worked a gig for Rudy Turnbull for three nights, and then Rudy fired him."

"Fired him? What for?"

"For pulling a gun on a guy who showed more than a passing interest in his girlfriend's legs."

Jack sat silently mulling this over.

"If you ask me," she continued, "it was mostly her fault. I think she was testing him. Know what I mean?"

Jack thought that he did but shook his head and smiled into her green eyes.

She gave her hair a flick, shifted her tray, and changed her stance so that her blue-clad knee pressed lightly against his leg. Jack pretended that he didn't notice but was surprised to feel a glimmer of heat somewhere behind his navel. He considered it hopefully, not because he was ready to act, but because he hadn't felt any heat there for a long time.

"Like, she wanted to know how far he would go to "defend her honor" or some such. You know?"

Jack nodded. He did know. He remembered a similar situation back when he and Sarah had first been together. Jack hadn't had a gun, but he hadn't needed one. He remembered the soreness of his hands and the difficulty he'd had holding a hammer for a couple days afterward. His father had still been active on the crew then and had reminded him gently at the end of the week that a bar fight almost never had a winner, only losers. It was advice that Jack had taken to heart. He hadn't thrown a hand in anger since.

He ordered a beer and watched the waitress walk to the bar. She was wearing a long, open white blouse over bright-blue spandex. The blouse was gathered at the waist with a silver and turquoise concho belt so that all but a couple of very strategic inches of her firm and sleek blue legs were visible. His own interest in these particular legs was only in passing, but he took comfort from the fact that there was any interest at all. Lately there had been no interest in anything. It wasn't

44

so much interest even with Lisha. That was obligation and a deep sense of rightness, a completion that gave him a definite mooring place in the world. But his numbness showed in his inability to muster any emotion beyond a dispirited self-pity. Feeling himself quicken as he watched the taut-and-flow of his waitress as she moved about the room was like returning to consciousness from a coma of indeterminate length. He felt a tugging at some long-asleep muscle in his face. It was his first private smile in months.

She brought the beer and put it on a little napkin in front of him.

"You want me to start a tab?"

"No thanks. I won't be around long," he said, remembering the warmth of her against his thigh. "Say, you wouldn't have any idea where this trumpet player went after he got fired, would you?"

"No, honey, I've no idea."

She cocked her head so that her hair fell in a sparkling red curl over her arm as it held her tray.

"You're really looking for the girl, aren't you?"

Jack felt himself blush, but he met her eyes and nodded.

She pursed her lips and let her eyes focus on something that wasn't in the room. She reached into herself and pulled out a decision, straightening her head as she did so.

"Do you mind my asking why?"

Jack suppressed the urge to squirm in his chair. He looked at her nose with its dusting of faded freckles and then at her chin, which had just the hint of a cleft. Finally, he reached up with his blue-denim eyes and looked at her.

"I just want…" He paused, groping. "I need to say good-bye."

She cocked her head again, her eyes searching his, for what, Jack couldn't tell. They looked deeply into him, but it wasn't an uncomfortable examination. Finally, she nodded.

"You should talk to Rudy, the guy who did the firing. He'll be in here tonight, later. If you promise not to go charging off, at least not until I get off work, I'll point him out when he shows up."

Suddenly, she forced a quick laugh and turned her face away. "This is nuts," he heard her say.

"Look"—it was her turn to blush—"I don't do this. I don't make dates with strangers. But, well, you're not the usual cowboy who comes in here and stares at my boobs and says cute things like 'Whoa, babe, let 'er buck!'"

Jack felt another smile grow on his wide, craggy face.

"I was staring at your legs."

"I know."

Both of them felt a bit of the same heat now. They stared at the relative space above each other's head.

Jack took a deep breath.

"Yeah. Okay. I'll hang around. What time do you"—he caught himself in time to avoid the unfortunate sexual pun—"are you finished?"

"Nine o'clock." The words came out in a rush. Her pupils were huge, turning her green eyes into black pools that seemed capable of absorbing everything in the room.

"I guess I'll go get a bite to eat," he said, standing up. "Any place close you'd recommend?"

She nodded up at him.

"You could eat here, but I'd be lying if I told you that you couldn't do better across the street at Happy's. The food here's mostly for people who need to eat."

"Thanks."

He turned to go and then stopped and held out his hand.

"I'm Jack."

Her hand felt warm and smooth in his.

"I'm Willy."

46

"Willy?"

"Short for Willimina."

He grinned. So did she.

They shook hands, and Jack turned and walked out the door.


When he returned to Lefty's, he was surprised to be confronted with a cover charge. The guy at the door was big and friendly, all chest and arms and a smile as big as he was.

"Howdy, pardner, that'll be three bucks."

His shirt collar had bright silver points, and Jack would've bet a week's pay that his boots were fancied up with silver toe pieces. His hat was imitation felt, but the smile seemed genuine enough.

"I'm only going to be inside for a little while. What time does the music start?"

"Nine thirty. And it don't matter how long you stay—the cover's three bucks."

The smile was still genuine but wasn't quite as wide as it had been. Jack scratched his head and looked at the veins in the doorman's forearms.

"Look, I just want to get inside for a minute. Willy's going to introduce me to some guy, and then I'm outta here. Hey, I'm all for supporting your local musician, but I'll be long gone before the music even starts." He smiled hopefully.

The doorman stood up from behind his suddenly very small table. He looked eye to eye with Jack, something he probably wasn't used to doing with many people. There was still the trace of a smile.

"You say Willy's expecting you?"

"Yeah."

The doorman turned and spoke with the smaller man who had come to stand next to him.

"Go ask Willy if she's waiting for some guy named…" He turned

47

his head.

"Jack," said Jack.

"Jack," finished the doorman.

The other man exchanged a wide grin with the doorman and disappeared into the room. He came back a few moments later with a very puzzled look on his face.

"Yeah. She says she's been waiting for him."

The room had filled considerably during his sojourn across the street.

"Jack! There you are. C'mon, Rudy's over in a booth."

She tucked Jack's arm under her own and led him into the room.

"Thank you, Randy," she called over her shoulder to the doorman.

Jack couldn't help himself and smiled at the doorman too. If life had been a cartoon, there would've been a question mark over Randy's head as he stood open-mouthed watching them.

Willy introduced him to a whipcord of a man with a walrus mustache who was seated in a corner booth close to the stage at the far end of the room. The woman next to him looked like she studied both Vogue and Rolling Stone to no real advantage. Jack couldn't make heads or tails of what she was wearing, only that it was probably supposed to be in style this week. Rudy was dressed in an understated brown suit with a western cut, a gemstone bolo tie that complemented a yellow cowboy shirt with brown piping, and ostrich-skin boots. His hair clearly was his signature, though, and gave the impression of something between Lyle Lovett and Bart Simpson. He looked bored, which Jack figured was how he meant himself to look.

Willy finished the introduction in a rush and said she'd return as soon as she could.

"Remember, you promised," she said to Jack.

"I'll be here."

Rudy looked comfortable with the silence between them, something

Jack was not. He was grateful when Rudy broke the ice.

"Willy tells me you're looking for Peterson, the trumpet player."

"That's right. I was hoping you could give me a clue as to where he might have headed."

"Steal your woman, did he?" Rudy's grin was sudden and bright, like the flash of a piranha.

Jack let a little smile play with his mouth and made sure that his hands stayed quiet and relaxed. The woman, across from him in the confines of the booth, seemed to wake up. She unfolded her awareness like a bat unfurling its wings.

"You could say that, I guess." Jack nodded.

"Call it what you want." Rudy shrugged, lit a long tan cheroot, and looked at Jack through a veil of blue smoke.

Jack looked back. His gaze was level and blue. Rudy saw something there and got to the point.

"They went to Vegas. I heard him talk about a joint called Lucky Linda's somewhere off the Strip."

Jack nodded.

"And if"—he paused as Jack's eyes bored into him—"when you find the son of a bitch," Rudy went on, "tell him he'd best steer clear of here. There's folks who'd love to feed him to the coyotes a piece at a time. Fact is, friend, you'd please those folks greatly if you'd just drop-kick him into Lake Meade."

"Oh?"

"Aside from the absolute stupidity of pulling a gun on a regular, he skipped town and left some unpaid tabs behind. Taking advantage of people just doesn't cut it in our little community here. It just isn't healthy." He let twin streams of smoke filter through his mustache. "Know what I mean?"

Jack nodded. It was his turn to be bored, and he stifled a yawn. He was tired of tough guys and maybe just plain tired as well. He slid himself to the edge of the booth and stood up.

"Thanks. I'll pass along the message."

Rudy dismissed him with a wave and concentrated on his smoke. The woman had folded back into her silent cocoon. Jack left them to their separate togetherness and looked for Willy. He finally spotted her by the door talking to Randy the doorman. He yawned hugely as he walked over toward them.

Willy met him with an amused expression.

"Keeping you up?"

Jack managed a sheepish grin and ran a hand through his thick dark hair.

"It's past my bedtime, and tough guys make me sleepy. I'm not used to this wild life."

Randy snorted and looked at Willy as she looked at Jack. Her eyes were just a little glassy, and her color was high.

The western sky was a strange wash of pastels as the sun melted into the ever-present smog bank that held the entire valley hostage. The soft fading light turned Willy's hair to burnished copper and painted a ruddy glow on Jack's tanned face. They were very careful not to touch as they strolled along in a silence that was companionable, if not exactly comfortable.

Cars were turning into the parking lot in increasing numbers, some holding one or two people, some holding a crowd. A yellow Dodge came roaring in, music howling through the open windows and shot down the row where they were walking. Willy moved into Jack as the car shot past. Instinctively, Jack put an arm around her and left it there. Willy moved against him for a moment and then pulled away.

"This is crazy," she said.

Jack nodded slowly.

"If you're as amazed as I am," he said, "then you're truly amazed. I woke up this morning like every other morning for the past few months, empty and aching and feeling sorry for myself, when something happened. I'm not sure what, but something did. I got into a silent conversation with my five-month-old daughter, and whap! Here I am in a strange town on some kind of bizarre quest to reconnect to something, probably myself. I get confronted by a wide slab of muscle about a woman I don't even know who introduces me to a little knife blade of a fellow who'd cut your heart out just to show his girlfriend what it looks like. Then I find myself walking through a sunset with the woman I just met, who may just be one of the prettiest people on the planet, sometimes feeling like I've known her for years and sometimes feeling like a school kid. I gotta tell you, Willy, if it wasn't for this weird sense of calm, I'd be totally discombobulated."

They looked at each other, both surprised at Jack's outburst. A little smile wrinkled Willy's eyes.

"What else are you thinking?"

Jack took a deep breath and sighed, too embarrassed to say anything else.

"What? C'mon, Jack, tell me."

He put his hands on his hips and stared at the ground.

"C'mon." She took his arm and tucked it under hers so that he could feel the underside of the sleek swell of her right breast.

He stopped staring at the ground and looked at her.

"That's cheating," he said.

She threw back her head and laughed and held his arm tighter. Jack caught himself grinning.

"I was wondering why a person like you was...unattached."

Willy's smile faded to a familiar worn sadness, but she didn't relinquish his arm.

"My husband was killed about a year ago. We had worked our place hard for five years. We had just dragged the ends together so that they met when a hay truck turned over on him, and it just about killed me too. I owe a lot to Randy, and other friends too. They got me through a real tough time, hopefully the toughest time of my life. I haven't dated anyone since Steve died."

Her grin came back, stole across her face, and lighted it from the inside so that it seemed to glow. Her hair held and magnified all the fading light in a molten aura surrounding her head.

Jack looked at her almost dumbfounded. He had only a vague awareness of their surroundings, of the bustle and flash of a big town just as darkness settles.

Part of him felt like he should turn and run. Instead, he put out his free hand and touched her hair.

"Just what color is your hair, anyway?"

Willy let go of his arm and caught his hand between both of hers. They stood for a moment watching each other like they were afraid to move for fear of seeing their private visions disappear.

"Are you staying anywhere?" she finally asked.

"No. I was figuring to push on."

"Let's go to my house," Willy said. "I think my couch is long enough to accommodate most of you. Then I'll fix some breakfast, and you can get a fresh start in the morning."

He followed her up Chester Avenue, turned behind her onto China Grade, and finally headed up the Kern River on Round Mountain Road. They drove past the entrance to the state park to a rambling ranch-style house that looked to have some land around it. Jack stood uncomfortably on the front porch while she opened the door. Once inside, he looked around at the comfortable front room and sat down on the wide well-worn couch.

"Make yourself at home," Willy called from around a corner and down a hall. "I'll be out in a minute."

He could hear water running. After a while, she called again.

"Why don't you make some coffee?"

Glad for something to do, Jack went to the adjoining kitchen, found the makings, and got the coffee maker going. The water had just started moving when Willy came into the room.

She had changed from her bright-blue leotard and long white blouse into an emerald-green nightdress that had three open buttons at her throat and stopped at mid-calf. Her face looked freshly scrubbed, which made her look younger and older at the same time. She perched on the edge of the wooden rocker across from him and hooked her bare feet behind the legs where they met the rocker blades. She didn't speak as he looked at her. As the silence grew, he found himself relaxing instead of growing more tense, which he found curious.

The coffee maker burbled, and she stood up.

"Black?"

He nodded.

As she moved into the kitchen, he kicked off his boots and settled in at the far end of the couch, so he could watch her. She hesitated briefly before choosing two mugs from the cupboard and put them on the counter. Then she looked out across the open counter at him.

"I'm going to have a little whiskey in mine. You want some?"

"Sure."

He watched her pour a strong shot into each cup. She came back into the front room, concentrating on the mugs in her hands and handed him one. Then she carefully sat at the far end of the couch, tucking her legs under her while holding her mug in both hands.

Jack took a sip of his coffee. The bite of the whiskey in it was strong.

"Jesus, lady. You trying to get me drunk?"

Her smile was open. "What I'm trying to do," she said after sipping from her own cup, "is figure out what the hell you're doing here."

"Well, if it's any consolation," he said while leaning back, "I'm kind of wondering what I'm doing here too."

They sipped in silence for a bit, and then Willy stretched out her legs so that her feet were touching his.

"Want to tell me about it?" she asked.

He took a long pull at his mug, draining it. He looked at the bottom of the cup and put in on the table that fronted the couch. Then he leaned back again and closed his eyes.

Willy was patient. She got comfortable and tucked her nightdress around her legs. Finally, she heard him take a deep breath, and she saw him open his eyes.

"Yeah. I do," he said.

So, he did. He told her about the night he and Sarah met, how he'd been in LA and she'd been dancing in a joint on Sunset. He'd been as transfixed by her perfect body as she'd been taken with his small-town ways and his total concentration. He'd been open and honest, and she had responded to him. He hadn't tried to be cool or pretend that he wasn't affected by her posing.

After a couple of months of visits in LA, they started to date, casually at first. After another month of progressively serious dating, he persuaded Sarah to leave the big city and move in with him. He offered her the chance to give up on the starlet routine and concentrate on her other interests, which were modern dance and art history. He paid half of her tuition at the local community college, and she took to it. Everything seemed in tune until she ran out of her own money. It was shortly after she became dependent upon him financially that her Van Gogh obsession showed up, that first winter they were together.

Willy, quiet at her end of the couch in rapt attention, then heard about the business with the ear and of other smaller clues, some of them Jack was realizing for the first time with the telling. He found himself reliving the happiness that had been and also the consternation and mounting despair as things had begun to unravel.

Then came the hard part.

After they had learned of her pregnancy, Sarah had retreated into a shell. At first, he put it down to her trying to accept the situation and figured that she was busy getting in tune with this new aspect of herself. He proposed marriage, but she refused and retreated more deeply into herself. By the time Lisha was ready, Sarah and Jack were hardly speaking.

Sarah hadn't had an easy time with the labor, and before it was over, the doctor put her under. When she woke, she was listless and uncommunicative and remained that way even after she and Lisha came home from the hospital. Within a month after the birth, while Jack was at work, she left Lisha with Eunice and was gone.

Jack had been hoping that the post-partum depression, or whatever it was, would disappear after time and that they'd become the family he'd desperately wanted them to become. But it was not to be, and here he was in Willy's front room, after four months of solitude and self-pity, awakening again after an enforced sleep.

After the lingering vibrations of his voice died away, Jack stood awkwardly and went toward the kitchen for more coffee.

"Me too?" Willy held out her cup.

He looked into her eyes briefly, then away, as he took the cup. He thought he saw anger there and didn't know what else to say. When he returned with the coffee, Willy had her arms folded across her chest, so he put the cup on the table.

"That's just as it should be," he said.

"What?"

"Coffee on the coffee table. I mean, I guess that's why they call them coffee tables."

The stiff line of her mouth softened, but she didn't smile. Jack sat down on his end of the couch and stretched out his long legs. Willy sat up and tucked her legs beneath her.

Jack threw his arms back over his head and stretched until he felt the tension from telling the story begin to leave. He yawned, remembering to cover his mouth only after he was mostly done. He felt light-headed, some of it from the whiskey, but mostly from finally getting it out, putting what he felt into the air for another person to hear.

He looked at Willy. Her face was mostly closed. Tiny lines showed at the corners of her eyes and mouth. A faint furrow had tightened the skin of her forehead. Jack suddenly knew that he was looking at her true face, the face that had come to live upon her since the death of her husband. A sense of intense kinship grew in him. He didn't know exactly, but he thought it might be like what a miner felt as the first shaft of light split the darkness after a cave-in.

"You're angry," he said.

Willy shook herself away from some private place and looked at him. When their eyes met, the lines in her face deepened.

"I can't help it," she said. "To bring a child into the world and then just disappear is totally irresponsible. Oh, I can understand it well enough. She didn't abandon her. No. She abandoned you. To her, the child was of no consequence. You should be relieved that she left the baby with you."

"She just couldn't handle it."

"No, she couldn't. It's not at all like a mother who puts her child up for adoption. That requires courage; it's up-front. It's taking that initial responsibility for the welfare of the child. In that situation, the child is put first or, at the very least, on equal terms. In Sarah's case, she just turned tail and ran. What a sad, sorry bitch."

They were silent for a moment.

"It's funny," Jack said. "For a minute there, I felt like I should defend her."

"Don't you dare!"

"No. I don't reckon I will."

Jack leaned forward and took a sip from his cup. When he put the cup down, Willy was next to him. She put her arms around him as he leaned back. She fit her left hip into the hollow of his waist and rested her head upon his chest. He put his right hand over the soft warm green of her shoulder. After a few minor adjustments, they lay very still and listened to each other breathe.

After a long time, Jack thought he opened his eyes and saw a man in the room looking at them. He tried to get up but was held fast against the couch. There was no sense of danger, and the man, wearing faded worn Wranglers and a plaid shirt with pearl buttons, grinned at him.

Then Willy was shaking him gently, and he came awake.

"Jack, come on. Let's go to bed. We fell asleep."

He sat up and looked around the room. Willy was smoothing her hair and tugging at his arm. Slowly he followed her down a hall and into the bedroom.

She went into the bathroom, and he would have followed her right in if she hadn't closed the door. Without thinking, he got undressed and crawled into the bed. The sheets were cold against his skin.

Willy climbed in next to him and snuggled close. She smelled of toothpaste. The sheets warmed. Jack noticed that the heat he'd felt back at the bar was still there, but it kept a distance, like a fog bank hanging just offshore. His mind had yet to keep up with his physical arousal. The phrase "early to rise…" came to him, and he smiled into the dark.

Jack unwrapped the mystery of Willy's molten core a gasp at a time. Her breath caught and held, caught and held, until the first ripples of her release began. Then she drew him into her until there was no place for either of them, except each within the other. He rolled to his back and breathed through the sweetness of her breasts as she rocked against him. The ripples became a torrent roaring down a desert arroyo, snapping nerves and synapses, carrying everything in its path to an immensity of need. It gathered and swelled and finally shot from the edge of their loneliness and fell and fell until the planes of their awareness shifted, rotating their horizon until gravity surrendered. The chrysalises that had become so familiar burst, and they were able to unfold their damp wings. They became creatures of flight and direction. They remembered how, soaring, finding thermals to ride, enjoying the new view, crying like children and then laughing through the tears. They landed together and blessed the magic of the world—they were the magic of the world. When their strength was scattered beyond what they could muster, they slept.

Jack knew he was dreaming but was powerless to stop it. The air was so full of dust that he could taste it. His eyes watered, and he wondered if he'd been crying, because his face was wet. There was a hollow repetitive dripping noise, and he searched for its source. Looking down, Jack saw that something indeed was dripping onto his boot. He stooped to examine it and felt an electric rush when he realized that it was blood.

Jack snapped awake and lay listening to his heart pound. Light was streaming into the bedroom through the eastern windows. He put out an arm for Willy, but she wasn't there. Moving stiffly, he swung his legs over the edge of the bed and put his feet on the floor. He hadn't slept this late in years. It felt dangerous to him somehow, like he'd violated a cardinal rule.

Willy sat in the kitchen dressed in faded black jeans and a well-worn maroon sweatshirt that read UNLV across the front. She held a coffee cup with both hands as she stared out the window to the northeast. The soft morning sun on her face showed the furrows in her brow. She didn't say anything as Jack rinsed out his cup from the night before and poured himself some coffee.

"Good morning," he said and kissed the back of her head.

"Good morning."

He felt her flinch ever so slightly and didn't try to kiss her again. She didn't look at him, and the kitchen seemed to shrink. As the expressive silence grew, Jack retreated to the living room and sat on the couch. As he sat down, the tightness that had been forming in his chest clamped down hard so that he stood up again almost immediately.

He moved to the window. His truck was sitting right where he'd left it.

"What's the best way back to I-15?" he called to the kitchen.

"Oh, back the way you came until you see a sign. It's easy."

The words tried to fill the silence but were engulfed quickly, like dust motes sucked through an open door. Jack shivered. There was something moving in him, something that was trying to fill the emptiness, but he couldn't quite find a way to give it the power it needed. He felt a sharp fear of loss, not like the endless dull ache he'd grown used to, but a sudden flame of anger and denial.

Breakfast was prepared and eaten. Dishes were carried to the sink. Jack went out to the truck and got a toothbrush out of his overnight bag. As he walked back to the house, he saw a long smudge of cloud above the desert horizon to the east.

His belly was full but still felt empty. He tried to think of Lisha and bring a sense of wholeness back to him but even she seemed a long way away. When he moved through the living room, he noticed that Willy had returned to her vigil by the window.

"Mind if I steal a lick of toothpaste?"

"Go ahead. In the right-hand drawer."

When he was finally ready to go, he stopped behind her in the kitchen. He put his hands on her shoulders. She didn't flinch this time, but she didn't respond either.

"Hey. Walk me to the door."

Willy turned and attempted a half smile that got stuck in her mouth and never bloomed.

On the front porch, Jack put his hands on her shoulders again and felt her stiffen as she raised her arms to push them away.

"No. Please."

Jack looked at her but could only see the surface of her eyes. The green looked through cataracts of distance and seemed pale.

"Thanks," he said. "You're a very special person. When I get through with this, could I come back and see you?"

Willy nodded and looked at the ground.

"Bye."

Jack turned and walked to his truck, boots unnaturally loud on the gravel of the driveway. The truck started with its customary roar and he was backing up to turn around when the feeling of fullness came back to him. He looked back at the house. Willy was leaned against a porch post, and Jack couldn't tell if she was looking at him or not. He tried a small wave, and she nodded her head. For a moment he sat listening to the motor idle. Then he dropped it into gear and rolled forward onto the road.

The two-lane northbound concrete rose gently but steadily toward the horizon. Jack watched the darkness of the storm gathering ahead of him and felt a thrill as lightning danced on the great bare shoulders of the mountains. An occasional bucket-sized raindrop dashed against his windshield. Jack had driven through many a desert rainstorm and knew that in an instant he could be moving through an aquarium.

On both sides of the pass ahead he could see the mountains blur where the rain fell heavily, blotting out the distinction between sky and earth. Cars coming from the other direction had their headlights on and looked as if they needed to shake themselves like brightly colored dogs come in from the backyard.

Another couple of miles and he was in it. A giant hand slammed down on the truck and almost drove the air out of his lungs. The wipers barely cleared his vision. The wind threw waves of water and then small rocks and bits and bunches of plants. In one brief violent gust, Jack thought a small lizard skittered across the hood of the truck, but he couldn't be sure.

A wide, crooked smile transfixed Jack's face, and after a while, he couldn't help himself. He broke into song and harmonized loudly with the storm. He figured that his free-form performance might not be ready for the big time, but he knew that the songwriter had impeccable credentials.

Jack was almost sorry when he crested the last rise of the pass and left the storm there, howling out another verse for the travelers still to come.

The truck rolled down the long hill on a cloud of mist, praising gravity instead of cursing it. Before long, the first casinos started shouting from the roadside. Jack, feeling strangely refreshed, ignored them and pulled off the freeway at Tropicana Boulevard. He passed the fantasy turrets of the Excalibur and turned left onto the Strip. At a little T-shirt shop on the right, he saw a phone booth.

Lucky Linda's was on Decatur near the intersection with West Sahara. Ten minutes later he was walking into the small casino. As he stood trying to get himself acclimated to the ringing din and flash of the rows of gleaming slots, a jackpot bell near him went off. It was accompanied by the excited whoops of the winner.

Jack turned to see whose luck had come to visit, and his heart caught briefly before lurching back to its steady beat. The winner was Pete Peterson.

His eyelids snapped up, and he caught himself looking for Sarah. Jack felt the almost-forgotten hole yawn with a vengeance around him, nearly driving the last several hours from him completely. How stupid he'd been to think that this ridiculous journey would do him any good, that he could reclaim himself from the morass of self-pity that had engulfed him. He wanted to pick Peterson up and shake him like a rag, grind the winner's smile from him and replace it with pain and fear. There was no way any of this could be made to give him hope, to show him how to rejoin some kind of life. Turning blindly, he made a move toward the door, thinking only to get back to his truck and disappear. His breath came in short bursts, and salt stung his eyes. The door was close now. He was almost through with this banal odyssey. What the hell had he been thinking? His mind was closing itself up, and macabre laughter echoed from the smooth featureless walls of the hole as it loomed around him. Holiday season was over.

But the tiniest of bubbles rose through the murk, oscillating under the pressure and expanding as it sensed the surface. When it popped at the top of his heart, he heard his daughter's imaginary voice.

"I need all of you, and so do you."

Jack stopped and ran a hand through the rich brown hair where it curled over his collar. He took a step back into the casino and forced his attention to Peterson again, whose expression was still one of rapt delight. Something in his lips showed that smiling was an effort for him, and it wasn't long before his pale angular face fell back into its normal guarded clench. Only his eyes stayed bright.

People along the row of machines where Pete stood looked at him with a mixture of envy and dislike. His luck had both given them hope and shriven them of the last desire to stop while they still had something to spend. Visions of reality could now pass again, invisible and unheeded, until the next jackpot reminded them of what they were here for. Something for nothing.

It was a lie, of course, but that was part of the game. Peterson hadn't even removed all the quarters from the yawning tray of the machine he was playing before he was, once again, just another body along a row of flashing lights.

Jack ignored the seductive promise of oblivion the hole was offering and walked down the aisle. Pete wore a mauve sport jacket over a dark-blue T-shirt. Jack wondered if the gun was there on his left hip, almost hoping that it was.

"Pretty good haul," he said.

Pete looked up from the large plastic bucket that he was scooping the quarters into. When he saw Jack, his eyes lost their bright flush and hooded themselves carefully. His right hand came up as he straightened and toyed briefly with his wide silver belt buckle.

So the gun was there.

"Hullo, Jack. What the hell are you doing here?"

Jack stretched his arms and felt an odd vibration along them. When it passed, he was strangely calm. He was in the chute now. There was no turning back.

"Just cruising. Got some time off and needed to get away. Las Vegas seemed like a good idea."

Pete looked at his watch. "You must've got outta town pretty early."

"Yeah, well, early to bed and early to rise…"

Peterson flashed a grin. "Yeah," he said.

They stood amid the noise and watched each other for a moment.

"Sarah's dancing again," Pete finally said.

"Oh?" Jack tried to sound noncommittal. "That kind of surprises me, I guess."

"Yeah, well she was getting kinda bored just hanging around all the time, so she checked out a place called Zook's, and they hired her right off. The money's pretty good. I've been looking for a good sit-down gig and finally got one here. So…"

"How long?"

"How long what?" Pete's eyes narrowed.

"The gig."

"Oh. Three months. I've played a couple casuals here, and the house band picked me up. I start the regular gig night after tomorrow. How long are you around for?"

"Just today, probably."

Silence fell between them again. Jack felt an undercurrent ripple through his calm. It knotted in his belly briefly before moving on. He stretched his arms again and, with some surprise, noticed that his hands were balled into fists. He saw that Peterson noticed it too. He looked down at his boots and felt a vague sense of disquiet.

"Look, Jack," Pete said. "I can't say I'm sorry that Sarah skipped out on you and the kid. She's a great lady, and I'm glad she's with me. But I didn't steal her from you, and you beating the shit out of me isn't going to make a bit of difference about anything.

It was Jack's turn to grin. "It might make me feel better, though."

Peterson took his bucket of quarters from where they rested on the padded stool in front of the machine and took half a step back. His feral eyes hardened as his fingers worried at his belt buckle again, but his voice softened. "What do want, Jack? You want her back?"

"Nope. All I really want is to say good-bye. I know it sounds strange, but that's the only way I can express it."

He could see that Peterson didn't believe him. But he didn't care. It was the truth.

"Tell you what," Pete said. "Why don't you run out to the trailer with me, and I'll see if Sarah wants to see you. If she does, you can make your pitch or whatever, and that'll be that. But don't get your hopes up. She's independent and wants to stay that way. I don't make any demands on her, and she likes that. A lot."

The undercurrent rolled through him again. Jack let his breath out very slowly through his nose. He wondered at the sudden magnanimity but let it go.

"Fair enough. Let's do it."

Jack followed Peterson's dusty gray Subaru out of town, heading north up the Tonopah Highway. The desert stretched beneath colossal thunderheads to the mountains on both sides of the broad valley, making each occasional housing development seem like an outpost on the moon. After only a few miles, the scattered neighborhoods thinned out to solitary houses that sat at arbitrary distances from the road. His sense of disquiet had settled into a dull throb that squeezed him somewhere between his gonads and the back of his neck.

Up ahead, he saw the Subaru turn off from the highway and disappear into the dust cloud of its own making. Jack slowed to a crawl as he followed. The boisterous storm back up on the pass that morning certainly hadn't dumped any water here.

Around a couple of dusty turns, he sensed, rather than saw, a widening in the dirt road. Sure enough, the Subaru was parked along side of a faded yellow house trailer that appeared, as the dust settled, to be in pretty good shape. Peterson was standing next to his car holding a mostly empty half-pint whiskey bottle as Jack got out of the truck.

Jack couldn't keep his eyes from searching the windows of the trailer. A face ought to materialize there, unless she recognized the truck and was hiding. He was trying to mask his anxiousness when Pete's voice put a short-circuit into his thoughts.

"Still got it bad, don't you, Jack."

He turned and stopped. Peterson had moved away from the car and was standing with his feet apart, looking right at his head, sighting down the barrel of the .38 pistol. From Jack's point of view, it looked like a cannon.

Right on cue, thunder rolled in the distance, and the wind did a fitful dance across the scrub brush. Jack disappeared into himself and listened to the wind. He felt he was in the very center of the long deep hole, a note trapped in a huge mystical flute. There was light above him, but he couldn't tell if it was from where he'd come or where he was headed. Then he felt a gathering breath, and the flute blew him free into the air. When the world re-formed around him, Peterson was still standing in the rising wind behind the pistol. Jack felt like an ice cube was being held against the middle of his forehead.

It started somewhere at the core of him and rattled around recklessly, a boomerang of emotion that would not be denied. He could only resist so long, and then he set it free upon his face. He grinned. It was a wide, craggy, lopsided, terrible thing to see. Peterson's eyes lost their self-assured heat and began to flicker. In all of his daydreams, he had been in a position just like this one, and now, instead of the fear he needed to see, he was face-to-face with a madman. This wasn't the way it should be at all. He was in control. He had the power.

"Don't do anything stupid, Jack!" His voice quavered and had gained an octave.

Jack's voice was quiet but could be heard above the rising wind. "You going to kill me, Pete? You going to shoot me dead?"

"You don't move. You stay right there or I'll—"

"You'll what? Pull the trigger and hope I drop? Why do you want to shoot me, Pete? You want to be a big man in Sarah's eyes? Hell, she's not even here, is she? In your own eyes? That's what this is all about, isn't it? Defending some bizarre mythical honor so you can walk tall in your own dreams and feel like you had what it took when things got rough. Let me tell you, Pete, it's a crock of shit. I just came to say good-bye. She owes me at least that much. Then I'll be out of here, and you can go back to whatever kind of life you had. It'll be a done deal. Don't screw it up, Pete. Shoot me, and your gig is history, your relationship with Sarah is history, your life is probably history."

Jack saw the gun waver and took a step. A part of him saw the wall of dust kicked up by the front of wind just before it engulfed them and they were both caught up in a whirling maelstrom of dust and debris. Jack turned to the side and angled in at where he'd last seen Peterson. They collided at the shoulder and went down in a tangle as the wind howled with glee.

Jack's right hand groped for the gun, but his head found it. Peterson chopped viciously at him with it, and Jack felt his scalp rip. With a roar that gave the wind a brief pause, he locked his hand completely around Pete's as it struggled to hang on to the pistol.

Peterson twisted around and drove his head into Jack's face. He tried it again but found himself caught in a vice of looping brown arms that tightened inexorably. He tried to twist free but only managed to wedge the side of his head against Jack's face. He could feel the blood from Jack's ruined nose running into his ear.

Jack's mouth was open as he tried to draw a breath. As Pete struggled to get away, Jack's teeth clamped onto his ear. For his part, Jack bit down as hard as he could.

Pete Peterson screamed, and it was over. Jack let go and watched him scramble away on his hands and knees, whimpering like a wounded cat. Jack spit and felt his stomach heave. He allowed himself to be sick. When he was finished, he noticed that he still had the gun locked in his right hand. Standing up slowly, he threw the pistol as far as he could out into the swirling dust.

Squinting against the stinging sand, Jack somehow found his truck and clambered inside. He rummaged around in his overnight bag and came up with a towel and did his best to clean up his face and stop the flow of blood from his scalp. His nose was a mess. Taking it between his right index and middle fingers, he yanked downward as hard and as straight as he could. The pain was immense, but he did feel an oddly satisfying little pop. Then the pain began to clear.

The wind was dying as the front moved on toward the mountains to the west. The air was still thick with dust, but visibility was slowly returning. Jack thought he could see Peterson huddled in a heap between his car and the trailer. Jack got out of the truck still dabbing at his face with the towel and went over to him.

Peterson heard him coming and curled up into a ball. His voice was muffled. "You stay away from me, you son of a bitch. You bit my goddamn ear off."

"Yeah. I did. And you have the mother of my child and pulled a gun on me. So maybe we're about even." Jack stood and looked down at Pete's heaving shoulders. "I didn't bust up your lips or anything. You can still play. Just get that thing cleaned up and wear you hair down. Nobody'll even know."

"Just get the hell out of here, you bastard."

"My pleasure."

Jack walked back to his truck. Before he got in, he called over his shoulder. "Hey, Pete, you ought to save that ear for Sarah. She'll probably get a real charge out of it." Then he added an afterthought. "Oh, and if I were you, I'd stay clear of Bakersfield."

On the way back to town, he stopped at a filling station and managed to get into the men's room without anyone seeing him. He stared at his milky reflection in the faded mirror as he waited for the water to get as cold as it would. Both eyes would probably be black in a couple of hours. He'd better get moving.

After he'd cleaned himself up, he dug out a fresh shirt but didn't put it on. He wadded up some paper towels and pressed them tightly to the rip in his scalp. To keep them in place, he pulled on a long-since-new baseball cap that read, In It 2 Win It across the front.

He made one more stop at a motel at the edge of town and filled the towel with ice from what sounded like a washing machine full of broken glass. When he pulled into the parking lot at Zook's, he tossed the ice pack onto the floorboards and got out. He was beginning to feel human again. He checked his eyes in the side mirror as he buttoned his shirt. There was swelling around the bridge of his nose, but the color was still okay. Good. Maybe it wasn't as bad as he'd thought.

As he paid the cover charge at the door, Jack glanced over at the stage in time to see Sarah come through the curtains and walk into the lights. He felt an immediate ache when he saw her. It was as if someone had been repeatedly smacking his heart with a small bat. It wasn't a crushing all-pervasive pain, just a wide ache that exercise would cure.

Jack watched her move to the pulse of the music. She couldn't identify him in the darkness where he stood, so he moved closer to the stage. There were five or six men hunched around the perimeter, leaning on their elbows or nursing their drinks. When she looked up and saw Jack, her eyes widened and she almost stumbled, but she gamely did a pirouette to cover for it. Jack grinned at her but moved no closer.

After a couple of moments, it was obvious to the men sitting around the stage that their dancer was paying no attention to them. They shifted uneasily and turned to stare at the tall stranger standing in the light at the edge of shadow.

Jack had Sarah's undivided attention now. He savored it. When she finally summoned the courage and gave in to her curiosity, she came over to his side of the stage. Jack looked at her and felt the rekindling of those nights with the window open to the smell of the sea. He felt the heat of their ancient passion and remembered how the room would explode into streaks of light as the heavy tide would drag them into oblivion and the waves crashed them against each other until they were spent and all they could take in or move out was air.

He took a step toward her and drank in her scent. He let himself long for her perfect breasts and ache to taste the hollow of her throat.

Then he watched her smile that supple small smile that used to delight him with its promise. But instead of melting him and shaping him to her will, in it he saw his daughter. He calmed and felt his desire float into the air like the sound of a radio playing outside on a windy day. The weight he'd carried for too long fell from him in scattered liquid lumps.

He stepped back and offered her a smile of his own, one that held both relief and lost love and hinted at the difference he felt rise within him. He winked and blew her a kiss. Then, as her heart-shaped mouth dropped open and she stopped dancing altogether, he turned and walked out of the door into the afternoon sunlight.

The drive back to Bakersfield happened quickly. He pulled into the rough gravel driveway, watched himself shut off the motor, and walk to the house. It looked like somebody else's hand knocking on the door.

Suddenly, Willy was there looking at him.

"Oh you," she said. "You."

Then she was crying. Jack stood looking back at her and felt ready to burst. Neither of them would remember who moved first, but in a heartbeat they melded into a strong wrap of arms as each tried to absorb the other in a hug so fierce that the atomic structure of the universe held its breath. Time had no more meaning than the eyelash of a bat hanging in a cave at the center of the earth.

The kiss that followed was eloquent. When it was complete, it ended.

They grinned and tried not to snuffle.

"Not a dry eye in the house," she said.

"Yeah. These sappy movies get me every time."

She moved against him again and put her cheek against his chest.

"I can't stay," Jack said. "I've got to get home."

Willy stepped back and put a warm hand alongside his face.

"I know. That's the way it is. But you call me when it's right. You call. Then, when I can, I'll come see you. And your daughter."

Jack nodded. "Yes, ma'am." He grinned. "Should be sometime tomorrow."

She was deadly serious as Jack looked at the furrow in her brow. "Don't rush anything," she said. "We don't need to go fast. We should be scared to death."

Arm in arm they walked to the truck, which waited with the driver-side door hanging open like a jug-handle ear. This time the hug, not as fierce, was comfortable and full. When they let go of each other, the wind came up and ruffled their hair.

He climbed into the Chevy, shut the door, and rolled down the window. The last kiss was a simple period at the end of a paragraph, a brushstroke of color in a painting of the sunrise.

In his rear-view mirror, Jack watched Willy watching him until he was around a bend of road and gone.

He was about thirty miles south when he pulled in for gas. While his tank was filling, he found the pay phone and called Eunice.

"Eunice? This is Jack. How's my girl?"

His grin was so big that it pulled at the new scab on his scalp and made him wince. Then he grinned again.

"I'll be there to pick her up before dark."

## WHITE RAVENS

The brightness of the fog should hurt my eyes, but my pupils feel huge, like they have been starving for light. I wonder about this when the fog before me thins and I see a shape. The shape becomes a young girl of perhaps thirteen or fourteen with long braided black hair. She is wearing faded jeans and a white T-shirt that is too big for her. She is smiling at me. There is something about her that I want to recognize. Her smile is in her dark eyes, but they are somber too, like she has arrived at some great truth and found it only acceptable.

The fog moves aside now, but I can feel it surrounding us, off to all sides, quiet and bright. We stand on an open hillside in late-afternoon sun where the wind blows along the direction of the shadows. It ruffles my hair. I am momentarily annoyed because this means I have lost my hat. I mutter something, and the girl laughs. Recognition shoots through my belly as the sound bubbles around me.

"Missy!"

"Hello, Jack. It has come to this, and you still have that goofy smile. It is a good thing."

Her voice brings back long afternoons—watching the dogs work the sheep, their yips and whines becoming as understandable as conversation around a campfire as the summer wears on. On some mornings, the sheep would sound like a babbling marketplace crowd as they watched warily for the dogs. To me, it is no wonder that it was the shepherds in the Bible who heard voices.

For five years, she and I were together every day from midsummer to the first frost high up toward the Blues as we followed the sheep that her father, George Looking Hawk, tended for my father. I was supposed to be learning the sheep business, and she didn't have any place else to go. She and I would always be on the lookout for coyotes, and she took great delight in being a better shot than me. But I don't think there was ever an awkward moment between us. During those times, free on the high range scattered with dark stands of Lodgepole and Ponderosa, I never once ached to be anywhere else. But after that last summer, just before the first snow of the winter of 1965, after we'd brought the sheep into the low pastures, I was out in the woodshed splitting up kindling when George suddenly stood in the bleak light of the doorway.

"She's gone" was all he'd said.

"Gone? What do you mean gone? Did she run away? Is she lost?"

Then his eyes held me, and I knew. I remember the axe falling to the floor so that I had to jump to avoid the bounce.

"How?" was all I could manage.

George's eyes went to the floor.

"Wesley Budreau kicked one of the dogs. When she got in his face about it, he got interested in other things and beat her up 'cause she wouldn't..."

"Wouldn't? What..."

My sudden understanding sat me down on the chopping block. I had never thought of her that way, an object of...I didn't know what. My head spun, and my throat tightened. My hands curled into fists.

George looked at my hands.

"Wesely's dead too. Jimmy killed him."

That would be Jimmy Beans. He was a cousin or something. I

74

nodded.

George came to me and put a hand on my shoulder. He smelled of woodsmoke and dog and sheep. His other hand held something in front of my face. I tried to see it, but my eyes wouldn't work.

"She wanted you to have this."

When I didn't move, he stooped and pried one of my fists loose, the right one, I think. I felt him put something light and heavy at the same time into my open palm and gently close my numb fingers around it. His hand went back to my shoulder for a moment, and then he straightened.

"Ya-Tah-Hey," he said and walked out of the shed. I never saw him again.

The fog moves closer again, and I feel a twinge of regret. No fear, just a vague regret.

"Missy?"

"No, Jack, you're not. This is the between place, the place where you rest. You have to go back."

"There's nothing for me there."

Her smile is sad. "There is always something there, even if you don't know what it is. Sometimes it's just behind you. You can sense it's there and then turn to see nothing. Like white ravens."

"White ravens?"

"Just because you've never seen one doesn't mean that they don't exist. Maybe they're just behind you, just out of your knowledge."

The fog swirls around us, bright and warm. Missy begins to lose form, but I can still feel her sad sweet smile.

"Jack. You should find the necklace that my father gave you. It has power."

I want to ask, but I am gone.

There is a noise that I can't identify, a rushing humming sound whose amplitude rises and falls. Lights flash against my eyelids. They hurt my eyes. I hear voices.

"God, what a mess. Did the driver stop?"

"Nope. Probably thought he hit a 'possum."

I'm lifted into a white tunnel. The rushing noise goes away, and I try to make my eyes work. I think I can blink them.

"Hey. He's coming around. Can you hear me, mister?"

I blink some more. I think I see a face flash in a passing light. Someone is holding my arm.

"Whew. This one smells like sour grapes. That cheap wine probably saved his life, though. He must've been so loose when the car hit him that he stretched like a rubber band."

The image makes me want to laugh. Rubber Man. Oh yeah. I'm all stretched out. Suddenly, I'm tired, so I surrender to the backs of my eyelids.

For an older guy, they say, I heal pretty quick. The knee will never be the same, and I need dental work, but the rest of it is turning out okay. The Rastaman orderly tells me on the sly that they had to strap me to the bed because I got the shakes so bad. He asks me if he can sneak something in for me, but I say no because I don't want to owe him. The counselors are nice. They hum and cluck, and I nod and smile. Mostly I don't pay much attention, tell them what they think they want to hear, and drift off. But then it's the end of the line. The county, state, and federal funds are used up, and I'm waiting for the last visit in my new khaki pants and twill shirt. My old boots are too big, and my stained blue ski coat hangs on me like a condom on a car antenna. But someone has mended the tears, in my coat and sleeping bag both. The kindness warms me.

It's nice being sober, but it's scary too, and I don't think it will last very long. I'm starting to remember things long buried and can feel the old ache beginning. I can feel the buzz calling me, telling me to shove all these thoughts away. As long as I can keep moving, I say, maybe I can outrun the buzz. But maybe not.

Then she's there, calm, professional, enthusiastic. I listen for a while, and then I hear something that snaps everything tight. I interrupt.

"What did you say?"

"I said, Mr. Randall, that you need to empower yourself. You need to break this cycle of abuse that nearly got you killed."

"Empower. I need to empower myself?"

"Exactly."

"Thank you," I say. "Thank you for everything."

I grab my rucksack, get up from the green vinyl chair, and move through the lobby out to the street. My teeth ache. So does my knee.

The hospital is jammed into the side of a hill. The day is clear, and I can see the city stretch eastward to the foothills of Mt. Hood, who is shining white in the morning. I can see St. Helens' broken hump to the northeast as well. For a moment I allow myself to feel steadfastly alive, but it's something I don't want to waste, so I rein it all in to a small inside place where I feel it curl up to wait.

On my way to the train yard, I have to pass through some of my old haunts, but I luck out and don't see anyone I know. I feel like I've borrowed something precious and have to get it back before it's missed.

In The Dalles, there's a place I know, and I wash dishes for a meal. I also help myself to a few cans of clam chowder for later. It's expected, but I leave an IOU note anyway. In Pendleton I hang around the mill and ask for a ride down to Pilot Rock. Finally, a young guy with big dark sideburns says, "What the hell," and drops me at Stewart Road where he turns up to his double-wide.

From here it's a walk. The long golden hills swell up for miles until they break against the shadows of the Blues. At the market in the center of town, I trade in some pop cans for a pint of Tokay. The first night I sleep behind the shelter of an old rock corral that makes me feel young. The buzz is strangely quiet, and the bottle stays in my pack. Then I'm up and moving when the sky gives up its first light.

As I crest the first rise of the day, an old coyote lopes across my path. She pauses for a moment and looks over her shoulder at me, tongue lolling and ears up. I raise an imaginary rifle but don't pull the imaginary trigger. Instead, I drop my arms and call to her.

"Hey, old girl. We're not so different now."

She turns sideways to me and raises her muzzle, testing the breeze. Her yellow eyes seem to hold mine, until a pheasant crows from the wheat field below. Forgetting me, she trots off in the direction of the noise.

Long about midafternoon, I pause above the old homestead and wonder who's running it now. The house looks like I remember it, and the outlying sheds still look serviceable. My knee feels weak, but I push on.

Two more nights, and I'm here. I walk the last two miles and reach the tree line where the wind blows down the long afternoon shadows. It takes me a while to find the right tree. Two names are carved into the gnarled bark—no hearts, no arrows, just names. Over the years, the bark has just about closed mine up, but hers is still as clear as the pain in my knee.

I find a good sturdy stick and dig it up, an old ammo can we used to keep paint brushes in. The lid is rusted shut, and it takes me some time to open it. There it is, stuck to the bottom. With infinite care, I work it loose, and then it's in my hand, nothing special, just rusted fisherman's snap-swivels hooked together with a small delicate piece of turquoise hanging free. I hold it between my bent fingers, and the tears come. Finally.

When I'm done, I take the bottle and put it in the ammo can. It's a tight fit. Then I rebury it, just in case.

## ACKNOWLEDGEMENTS

Publishing a second edition of this collection was an idea that may or may not pan out. I've had mixed feelings about it. On one hand, I'm quite eager to include it in my own collection of contributions to American Literature. On the other, I fear it may be an exercise in futility. Such is the reality of the publishing world I find myself in. Having said that, I must also express my delighted amazement that the team at Word Hermit Press happily agreed to put *White Ravens And More Stories* out there in the ever changing climate of the publishing world.

I must also thank the following people:

Vinnie Kinsella for his work on the covers of the versions of this book; Andra Watkins for her tireless support and for setting an example of persistence; the authors who believed in the stories enough to offer the elusive blurb—I can't tell you how much that means to me; Kristin Thiel, whose editing helps illuminate what I'm trying to do; Toulouse, my grandpuppy, who patiently listened to all of my doubts and helped me put them into perspective; and as always, my soulmate Laura, who has taught me so much about persistent acceptance and what love really means.

## ABOUT THE AUTHOR

Jim Stewart lives in Gearhart, Oregon. He was born in the Midwest, lived near the New England coast, but has spent most of his life on the West Coast. His writing of place is an amalgam of the whole country. His writing of people is the same. His first novel, *Ochoco Reach*, is available in all the usual locations. Currently, he is writing his second novel, sketching his third, and planning his fourth. Life is good.